He Says Mars,
SHE SAYS VENUS

AN IRREVERENT GUIDE
TO RELATIONSHIPS

GW00503823

He Says Mars,
SHE SAYS VENUS

AN IRREVERENT GUIDE
TO RELATIONSHIPS

JASMINE BIRTLES
DR MARC BLAKE

BOXTREE

First published 2002 by Boxtree
an imprint of Pan Macmillan Ltd
Pan Macmillan, 20 New Wharf Road, London N1 9RR
Basingstoke and Oxford
Associated companies throughout the world
www.panmacmillan.com

ISBN 0 7522 6153 3

3 5 7 9 8 6 4 2

A CIP catalogue record for this book is available from
the British Library.

Design by Dan Newman/Perfect Bound Ltd
Printed by Bath Press Ltd, Bath

What's the difference between men and women? Well, if you're a woman, you'll be thinking of the first fifty or so; if you're a man, you won't be reading this. And if you're working at the *Sunday Sport*, you'll be thinking 'What are the optimum number of breasts we can get in this week's edition? And why do women only have two? And what's the point of men having nipples? Ooh, but they're quite fun, though...'

When he tells you he loves you, he's saying it for three reasons.

1. He feels guilty.

2. You told him to tell you.

3. He wants a blow job, or possibly

something illegal, even between consenting adults (potting the pink and brown?).

When she tells you she loves you, she's saying it for one reason: she wants you to say it back. *He Says Mars, She Says Venus* is a compendium of knowledge about the vast chasm (stop sniggering) between what we say and what we mean.

Why is there this communication problem? Hey, if we told each other the truth, the human race would have died out centuries ago. *He Says Mars, She Says Venus* - forget different planets, we're from different galaxies! (Stop thinking about chocolate, please, madam.)

She says: You're my first.
She means: . . . today.

He says: I'll call you.

He means: I might call you; I'll never call you for the rest of my life; You bore me rigid; I'll only call you if I can't find anyone better; You slept with me too soon; You wouldn't sleep with me; Where are my socks?; I've forgotten your name; I'm leaving the country.

She says: I'll call you.

She means: I'll call you.

She says: You don't bring me flowers any more.

She means: If you come through that door one more time without so much as a lupin I'll be out faster than you can say Interflora.

She says: Oh, please, let me pay half.

She means: I'm not sleeping with you.

She says: Chocolates! How thoughtful.

She means: Milk Tray! So you think I'm fat *and* cheap.

11

He says: I'd like to come shopping but I've got this report to finish.

He means: The big match is on and I've got a six-pack with my name on it.

He says: I only did it because she reminded me of you.

He means: I've fancied your sister for years.

She says: What do you do for a living?

She means: What do you earn for a living?

She says: Does my bum look big in this?

She means: Please say I'm sexy whatever size I am.

He says: I'm a native French speaker and talk fluent Spanish.

He means: I can get by in a French bistro and I talk fluent bollocks.

He says: I used to be a brain surgeon and I trained as an artist.

He means: I faint at the sight of blood and am a terrible piss-artist.

She says: She's got a really nice personality.

She means: She's pig-ugly and no competition to me.

He says: Let's meet for tea.

He means: I'm gay but I like being seen with attractive women.

She says: Let's meet for tea.

She means: I'm not sure if you're gay but if you're not I want to have your babies.

She says: I can cope with pain.

She means: I've had twins, I get a bikini wax every month and I've had all kinds of medical instruments exploring my nether regions.

He says: I can cope with pain.

He means: If I were kicked in the nuts I wouldn't cry.

She says: I'll love you for ever.
She means: Till death us do part.

He says: I'll love you for ever.
He means: Till someone better
            comes along.

Her nice gifts for a wife:
      satin lingerie,
      romantic weekend
      away, expensive
      jewellery.

His nice gifts for a wife:
      a food processor, talc,
      a Thighmaster.

Her SWM definition:
Single White Male.

His SWM definition:
Sneaking While
Married.

She says: Hey, nice shirt!

She means: Colour-coordinated and stylish? Must be gay.

He says: If I told you, I'd have to kill you.

He means: If I told you, you'd want to kill me.

He says: I have to travel a lot with my work.

He means: I'm married.

He says: Sometimes I'm away for weeks at a time.

He means: I'm married with kids.

She says: It's so nice to meet someone who's really interested in me.

She means: I'm married.

She says: Oh, age isn't important to me.

She means: I'm a gold-digger and I'm only interested in your will.

He says: Oh, age isn't important to me.

He means: I'm desperate and you should be too.

He says: In my work I rub shoulders with the rich and famous every day.

He means: I'm a bouncer in the West End.

Her definition of committed:
> staying with the same partner for the rest of your life.

His definition of committed:
> The men in white coats come and take you away.

Her definition of a sensible diet:
    eating enough
    vitamins, minerals
    and proteins to keep
    you healthy.

His definition of a sensible diet:
    only eating foods that
    are brown, yellow or
    red (e.g. a Big Mac
    and fries).

She says: We just don't talk any more.

She means: You just don't talk any more.

She says: You're so sweet!

She means: I wouldn't touch you with gardening gloves.

He says: I love you like a sister.

He means: I'm into incest.

She says: I love you like a brother.

She means: I've found someone else so I don't need you to fancy me any more.

He says: You're looking very well.

He means: I want to get in your knickers right now.

He says: I used to have a nose stud in college.

He means: I understand pain and I know how to buy jewellery. Take me.

He says: She's a lesbian.

He means: She wouldn't sleep with me.

He says: She's just a tart.

He means: She slept with me once but only because she was drunk and she hasn't spoken to me since.

31

He *says*: She's a prude.

He *means*: She wouldn't sleep with me.

She *says*: He's such a sweetie.

She *means*: He took me out for an expensive and romantic night out and didn't bat an eyelid when I didn't offer sex. And he's not gay!

He says: She's really smart.

He means: She laughed at all my jokes.

He says: She's a ball-breaker.

He means: She got promoted above me.

She says: I want a man who's kind and dependable. I'm sick of bastards.

She means: I want babies.

She says: I'm sick of renting. I want to own my own home.

She means: I *really* want babies.

He *says*: They're really putting the pressure on at work.

He *means*: I'm having an affair.

He says: Let's visit your mother. We haven't seen her in ages.

He means: I'm having an affair and feeling guilty about it.

He *says:*   Call me.

He *means:* I'm not that interested
             but you could be good
             for a shag.

She *says:*   Call me.

She *means:* I want to marry you
              and have your babies.

She says: Let's go on holiday together.

She means: I've tried everything else so maybe this will persuade you to marry me.

He says: It's been a long time. I thought I'd get in touch.

He means: I've just split up with my girlfriend and fancied a shag.

He says: You talk too much.

He means: You keep interrupting my monologue about myself.

She says: I've spent all day cleaning the house.

She means: I've spent all day cleaning the house.

He says: I've spent all day cleaning the house.

He means: I emptied the bins, threw away some old newspapers and washed some old pants that were actually pulsating on the floor.

She says: I've put on a bit of weight.

She means: I may be half a centimetre larger around the waist today.

He says: I've put on a bit of weight.

He means: I'm twenty-eight stone, I haven't seen my feet since I was seven, but hey, women love a big cuddly hunk like me.

She says: I'm fat.

She means: I'm ugly, useless, a failure and totally unattractive to men. I might as well top myself now.

He says: I'm fat.

He means: I'm fat.

Her definition of stimulating reading material:
A thought-provoking novel or self-help book.

His definition of stimulating reading material:
What Sports Car, Victoria's Secret catalogue, Big Jugs Monthly.

Her definition of social embarrassment:
Being caught with clashing shoes and handbag.

His definition of social embarrassment:
Being caught with coordinated shirt and elegant suit and branded gay.

He says: You don't look after me like you should.

He means: My mother thinks you don't look after me like you should.

She says: I need some retail therapy.

She means: My husband's having an affair.

48

He says: You don't own me, you know!

He means: I can't tell you where I've been because then you'd know I'm seeing someone else.

He says: I've got a Maserati 3.5R injection sports.

He means: . . . and a small willy.

50

He says: I'm an international communications executive.

He means: I work in a call centre.

She says: I believe in motherhood and I think the role of the housewife has been greatly devalued.

She means: I hate working for a living.

She says: I'm a PA in the music industry.

She means: I'm a groupie.

She says: I love children.

She means: ...so give me some now!

He says: I love children.

He means: ...and was recently cautioned by the police for it.

She says: The lines on your face make you look distinguished and sexy.

She means: You've got power and money – who cares about looks?

She says: Money can't buy
me love.

She means: But credit cards can
rent it for a while.

He says: If I said you had a beautiful body would you hold it against me?

He means: I'm wrinkly, sad and desperate and too stupid to think up a better line.

Her definition of GSOH:
> Good Sense of
> Humour.

His definition of GSOH:
> Great Sex Or
> Hand-job.

He says: Face it, the marriage has been over for a long time.

He means: . . . and I couldn't face ending it without someone else to go off with.

She says: We just don't have anything in common.

She means: You're so boring I'd rather have exploratory surgery without an anaesthetic than spend one more minute with you.

He says: I'm sorry. I tried but I'll never be as good a cook as you.

He means: No way am I doing my share of the cooking in this house.

He says: I just wanted to be with you tonight.

He means: I'm scared of being on my own.

She says: We ought to invite your brother more often. He must get lonely on his own.

She means: I fancy him like crazy.

She says: I'm staying the night with Susan. She's been so lonely since John left.

She means: I'm having an affair and I want you to find out.

She says: Oh, you know I don't understand money.

She means: I've spent so much on your plastic I'm surprised it hasn't melted.

She says: He's not my type.

She means: Until I've drunk my body weight in Malibu.

He says: She's not my type.

He means: She turned me down.

She says: I'm not telling you how many men I've slept with.

She means: Think of a number and triple it.

He says: I've slept with a few women.

He means: More than you think, less than I'm prepared to admit to, not all for money.

He says: I really need some space.

He means: With other women in it.

He says: That dress looks good on you.

He means: And so do the other six you tried on – let's get going!

He says: I love what you're wearing.

He means: So keep dressing like a tart.

He *says*: I'll always love you.

He *means*: I'm leaving the country.

She *says*: I'll always love you.

She *means*: I will keep a shrine to you long after all my friends think I'm completely insane.

70

She says: I am so over him.

She means: I am not over him so don't ask me again until six months have passed or at least two transitional boyfriends.

He says: It was only a fling.

He means: It was months of hot sex until you found out.

She says: It was only a fling.

She means: One night of extraordinary passion, one month of contraceptive guilt.

He says: Sorry, I was kept late
at the office.

He means: Sorry, I was kept late
at the pub.

He says: I believe in fidelity.

He means: I was lucky enough to get you into bed, let alone anyone else.

She says: Love is overrated.

She means: Can you see my pain? Here, just let me TEAR OUT MY HEART!

He says: I want to hear the three magic words.

He means: Bring more beer.

He says: I saw that in a magazine.

He means: I saw that in a specialist magazine which is illegal here and only available on subscription.

She says: You'll really like my parents.

She means: I want to marry you.

She says: You'll really like my best friend.

She means: If you fancy her more than me I will kill you and devour your internal organs.

She says: I'm so glad you liked my best friend/sister.

She means: I'm so glad she didn't fancy you.

78

He says: You're great. Let's move in together immediately.

He means: I am not a man. I am a religious fanatic.

She says: Can I leave my toothbrush and a hairdryer at yours?

She means: Oh, and the rest of my stuff?

She says: Your sound system's really cool.

She means: But it isn't staying in the lounge, matey-boy. Back bedroom if you're *lucky!*

She says: I think we need to talk.

She means: I need to psycho-analyse your every thought, word and deed while you play deaf, dumb and stupid.

He says: We'll talk about it later.

He means: Is never a good time to talk about this?

She says: Do you still love me?

She means: Even though I have cellulite and am turning into my mother?

She says: We're going to have a special event.

She means: You leave me now and the PlayStation gets it.

He says: I'm happy with our sex life.

He means: Hey – even President Clinton got oral sex! Get on with it.

She says: I don't really go brown in the sun.

She means: I am ashamed of my body.

He says: I've cut down on my drinking.

He means: During my sleeping hours.

She says: No ice cream or pudding for me.

She means: I'll be picking at yours, anyway.

She says: I'll just have a salad.

She means: Saving me 200 calories, which can now go on wine.

He says: No, I'm on a diet.

He means: I have guilty periods
between lager and
pies.

She says: I feel such a failure.

She means: I am a normal woman in her twenties.

He says: I feel a failure.

He means: Only a blowjob will get me out of this depression.

He says: I might just pop into that record shop.

He means: I haven't bought every CD, DVD or computer game in there yet.

She says: I'm just off shopping with the girls.

She means: I am depressed and am doubting my clothes selecting and purchasing skills.

He says: I want to do so many sexy things with you.

He means: Except that, down there.

She says: You make me feel so great.

She means: Pretty good so far – now get down there.

He says: It's never happened before.

He means: It's happened before.

She says: Can you get something from the chemist's for me?

She means: This is the real test.

She says: You'll get on like a house on fire with my brother.

She means: He's an arsonist as well.

She says: Tell me you love me.

She means: You never tell me
you love me.

He says: I love you.

He means: I have tried everything
else to get into your
pants.

97

He says: I didn't mean it when I said I loved you.

He means: Oh God I'm hyperventilating – mayday, mayday – turn back time.

He says: I love you, but I'm not *in love* with you.

He means: I no longer fancy you.

She says: I never loved you.

She means: I loved you right up until the point at which I found out what you were doing with my sister/boss/ best friend/mother/ pet hamster.

She says: This isn't working out, is it?

She means: Three weeks ago this wasn't working; now it's way beyond that.

He says: I think we should start seeing other people.

He means: I am.

She says: But you told me you loved me?

She means: Which I took as a legally binding contract until one of us dies.

She says: BASTARD (you left me).

She means: BASTARD (you beat me to it).

She says: Let's put a telly in the bedroom.

She means: Our sex life is officially over, unless we can spice it up with Robbie Williams on MTV.

He says: I'll be up in a minute.

He means: The minute after I stop masturbating to Channel X.

She says: Do I look OK?

She means: Say yes – or it's another hour of this costume drama.

He says: Do I look OK?

He means: Has the middle-aged spread disappeared overnight?

He says: Look, I think I know how to do a barbecue.

He means: Me discover fire. Me cremate meat. Ook ook!

He says: How old do you think I am?

He means: I think I look younger than I am.

She says: How young do you think I am?

She means: No pressure, but this one's on pain of death.

He says: I'm thinking of joining a gym.

He means: My doctor has diagnosed obesity and I need a paddle to lever myself out of the chair.

She says: I'm doing three aerobics classes a week.

She means: I'm doing the instructor three times a week.

She says: I'm giving up smoking.

She means: I'm smoking other people's for a month, panicking about the stone I'll put on and then going back to forty a day.

He says: I'll never drink again.

He means: Or until next Friday night, whichever is soonest.

He says: Grey hair is so distinguished.

He means: I hope you can't see the bald spot from here?

She says: I'm friends with all my ex-boyfriends.

She means: And they treat me like the vain shallow bitch that I am.

He says: I don't see any of my exes.

He means: None of them will agree to quickie no-frills sex.

She says: I really get on with men.

She means: I wear boots and show off my cleavage.

He says: I really get on with women.

He means: I'm gay.

He says: I love oral sex.

He means: I love receiving oral sex.

She says: Oops.

She means: You are not putting it in there *ever*.

He says: Look, sex will make your period pain better.

He means: I really need a shag.

He says: My wife doesn't understand me.

He means: My wife understands me.

She says: Men are only after one thing.

He says: And sometimes not even that.

She says: Men are impossible.

He says: We're inefficient, incompetent and unhygienic – oh and we like to be left alone as well.

She says: The sex is great.

She means: I'm letting him do this stuff to me until he's too weak to leave.

He says: I understand women.

He means: I understand girls.

He says: I don't think there's a glass ceiling for women.

He means: I can't see it from up here.

He *says:* I believe in feminism.

He *means:* As long as it gets me a shag.

He says: I just want to stay in with you tonight.

He means: With food cooked for me, free TV and free sex, why go out and spend money?

He *says*: I hate wearing condoms.

He *means*: Go on the pill.

She says: It's a bad time of the month.

She means: But if you do it, you'll get major brownie points.

Dr Blake is a graduate in psychology, social sciences and lying. Having studied the human condition for several years he finally diagnosed it as malignant – with a bit of a sniffle.

He has been a 'people watcher' for some time, and regularly goes around holding a pair of net curtains. He was also a phrenologist for a while, until he discovered that it means feeling bumps on the head. One of the few men who really understands women, he's actually not gay – but does like to dress up as a 'lady' on occasion and to prance about a bit. His cat is in therapy.

Dr Blake is in no way related to his evil twin, Caleb March. Oh no.

Jasmine Birtles is the author of several self-help books, including *Feel the Fear and Run Away*, *Controlling the Playground – Respect Through Conflict* and *How to Get Along With Absolutely Everybody*, which she co-wrote with her ex-husband who she hasn't spoken to since 1993. She also offers ground-breaking therapy for household pets and is the author of the internationally recognized reports on cat behavioural problems entitled *Getting In Touch with the Tiger Within* and *Affirmations for Cats Who Loaf Too Much*. Before becoming a therapist she was a major force in the music business, managing tribute bands such as *The Pretend Pretenders*, *The Surrogate Mamas and Papas* and *Take That From Behind*. The Birtles' family motto, *Dieu et mon Droit*, means 'God and I are right' – which explains a lot.